APARTMENT 4A

DEAD HELP

Book 3

PJ Gray

SADDLEBACK
EDUCATIONAL PUBLISHING

APARTMENT 4A: BOOK 1

OUT OF CONTROL: BOOK 2

DEAD HELP: BOOK 3

SADDLEBACK
EDUCATIONAL PUBLISHING
www.sdlback.com

ISBN-13: 978-1-62250-710-8
ISBN-10: 1-62250-710-X
eBook: 978-1-61247-961-3

Printed in the U.S.A.

21 20 19 18 17   2 3 4 5 6

AUTHOR ACKNOWLEDGEMENTS

I wish to thank Carol Senderowitz
for her friendship and belief in my abilities.
Additional thanks and gratitude to my family and
friends for their love and support; likewise to the
staff at Saddleback Educational Publishing for
their generosity, graciousness, and enthusiasm.
Most importantly, my heartfelt thanks to
Scott Drawe for his love and support.

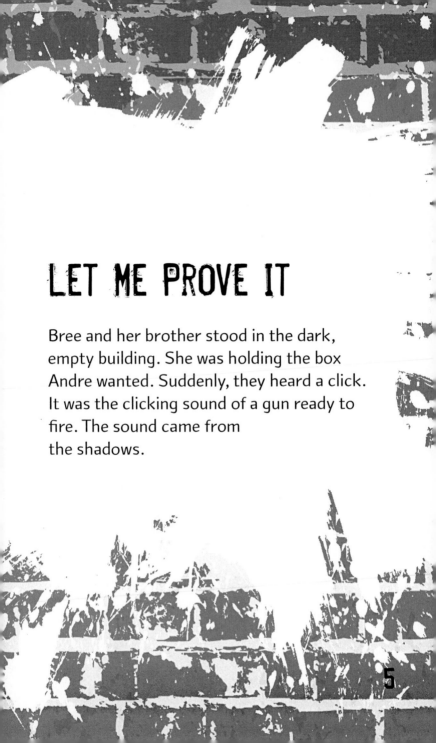

LET ME PROVE IT

Bree and her brother stood in the dark, empty building. She was holding the box Andre wanted. Suddenly, they heard a click. It was the clicking sound of a gun ready to fire. The sound came from the shadows.

Bree turned and saw the shadow of a person with a gun. She threw the box at the shadow. They heard the sound of the box hitting something or someone. Then they heard a gun fire as they ran to a window. Bree and Andre got out of the building.

They ran as fast as they could. They ran behind many buildings until they felt safe. They stopped in an alley to rest. Nobody was there. Nobody was following.

"Who shot at us?" Andre asked.

"I don't know," Bree replied. "Did anybody follow you to the building?"

"No, I came by myself."

They sat in the dark alley together. "What was in the box?" Andre asked softly. "Was it drugs?"

"No," Bree replied. Bree knew she was lying. She did not care. Bree knew her brother. She did not trust him. She knew he would do anything for money. She could smell the booze on him.

They tried to hear if they were being followed. "Why did you say you saw our mother?" Andre asked. "She's dead."

"I know, but I saw her," Bree replied. "I saw her in apartment 4A."

"What are you talking about?" Andre asked.

"Come back with me. I'll show you."

Just then, they heard a sound in the alley. Someone was walking very slowly. Bree and Andre made a run for it. They ran down more alleys. They took two different buses to get home.

DANGER COMES HOME

It was later that night. Bree and Andre got off at the bus stop near home. Andre had to buy a bottle at the store. He needed a drink.

They checked the mailbox when they got to the building. It was empty. Their aunt's monthly check was not there.

Bree and Andre stopped at the front door of apartment 4B. They looked at each other. They knew what each was thinking. Their aunt was dead. Life was going to be different now.

Bree and Andre turned and looked across the hall. They saw the front door of apartment 4A.

"Is the door locked?" Andre asked.

"I don't know," Bree replied. "Sometimes it is. Sometimes it isn't."

They walked over to the front door of apartment 4A. Bree turned the knob. The door was unlocked.

They walked in. It was empty and dark. There was light in the living room. It came from the streetlight outside the window.

Andre looked around the room. "This is where we lived with Mama," he said.

"And this is where I saw her."

"What did she look like?" Andre asked.

"She had long hair. She wore an old blue dress."

"I remember that dress," Andre said.

"Do you remember they called her Tutu?" Bree asked.

"Yes," Andre said. "I remember."

Andre walked slowly to the living room window. He took the last sip from his bottle. Then he threw it at the wall. Bree walked slowly to him. She put her hand on his arm. They stood there and said nothing.

Bree looked out the window. A car pulled up to their building. A man got out. It was her boss, Mr. Edwin. Then Mona got out. Bree saw Mr. Edwin holding Mona's arm. A gun was at her back.

Another man got out of the car. He stood next to it. He had a gun too.

17

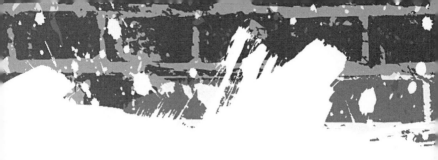

READY TO KILL

Bree and Andre saw Mr. Edwin and Mona enter their building. "That's my boss," Bree said. "He's got my friend."

"Bree, he's got a gun," Andre said. "What's going on?"

"I don't know. But he's looking for me."

"I'm done," Andre said as he moved to the front door.

Bree grabbed his arm. "You can't go," she said. "He's on his way up."

Andre began to sweat.

"The other man will shoot you if he sees you," Bree said. "And there may be others around the building."

"I only have a knife," Andre said.

"Listen carefully," Bree said. "I'll wait for Mr. Edwin and Mona in apartment 4B. I'll bring them here. You stab Mr. Edwin."

"How?"

"Wait behind the door," Bree said. "Then stab him when he comes in."

"He's got a gun. It won't work."

"Lock the door when I leave. Trust me!" Bree yelled.

Bree ran to apartment 4B. She called the police. "Hurry, please hurry," Bree said, holding the phone close to her mouth.

There was pounding on the front door. "Bree!" Bree did not move. "Open the door, Bree," Mr. Edwin called out. "Don't make me open it." Bree said nothing. Mr. Edwin kept at it. "I know you're there. I have Mona with me. She wants to tell you something."

"Bree, it's me," Mona cried. "Please let us in! Or he'll kill me."

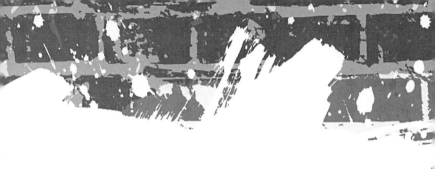

JUST IN TIME

Bree stopped at the door of apartment 4A. Mr. Edwin and Mona were standing behind her. Mr. Edwin had Mona in an armlock. His gun was pointed at Bree.

Bree hoped Andre was behind the door. She hoped Andre was ready to stab Mr. Edwin with his knife. She put her hand on the knob and turned it. The door was locked.

"Open it!" Mr. Edwin yelled.

"I can't," Bree replied. "I don't have the key."
Bree hoped Andre could hear her.

"Move!" Mr. Edwin yelled. He pointed his
gun at the door and shot the lock. Then he
kicked the door open. "You go first," he said
to Bree. "And no games."

Bree slowly walked through the door.
Mr. Edwin and Mona followed. "Where's
Andre?" Bree asked herself. "And where are
the police?"

"Where's the box?" Mr. Edwin asked. There
was a sound from the living room closet.
Mr. Edwin turned and shot at it. Bree and
Mona cried out. The closet door opened.
Andre fell onto the floor.

Bree stood in shock. Andre had been shot in the leg. He was holding it. Mr. Edwin clicked his gun and pointed it at Andre. He was going to kill him with one more shot.

At that moment, Mr. Edwin felt a cool wind on the back of his neck. He turned and saw a white cloud in the corner of the room. Inside the cloud was a woman with long dark hair. She was wearing an old blue dress.

MOMENT OF TRUTH

It was Tutu.

"Oh my God!" Mr. Edwin said. Mona cried out. Andre watched from the floor. His leg was bleeding.

"My poor baby," Tutu said with tears in her eyes.

Mr. Edwin shot at the ghost. Mona pushed away from him. She ran to Bree in fear.

The shot passed through Tutu. It hit the wall behind her. Mr. Edwin fired his gun at her again. The same thing happened.

Mr. Edwin dropped his gun. It hit the floor. Tutu's ghost screamed and ran at Mr. Edwin. "No!" he yelled.

Bree grabbed the gun.

"My baby! My baby!" cried Tutu's ghost.
She ran straight through Mr. Edwin. He fell
to the floor.

Then Tutu's ghost ran to the window and
jumped. Mona sobbed. The ghost melted in
the air.

Bree pointed the gun. She was ready to
shoot Mr. Edwin.

Mr. Edwin slowly stood. "Give me the gun,
Bree," he said.

"Don't move. Don't come any closer,"
Bree said.

Mr. Edwin took a step. "Okay, Bree," he said softly. "You can keep the gun. Just give me the box and I'll go."

"I don't have the box," Bree replied. "I mean it! Don't move or I'll shoot!"

"Where's the box?" Mr. Edwin asked.

"I delivered it to the building on Pine Street just like you asked." Bree hoped to hear the sound of a police car. "I called the police," Bree said. "They're coming right now."

"No, I don't think so," Mr. Edwin replied. He had a cold smile.

Mr. Edwin took another step. Mona was next to her. Andre was still on the floor, bleeding. He was in pain and could not get up. Bree pointed the gun at Mr. Edwin. She clicked it.

Then a man stepped into the room from the front door. He was Mr. Edwin's driver. The man drew his gun. He pointed it at Bree. He was ready to shoot.

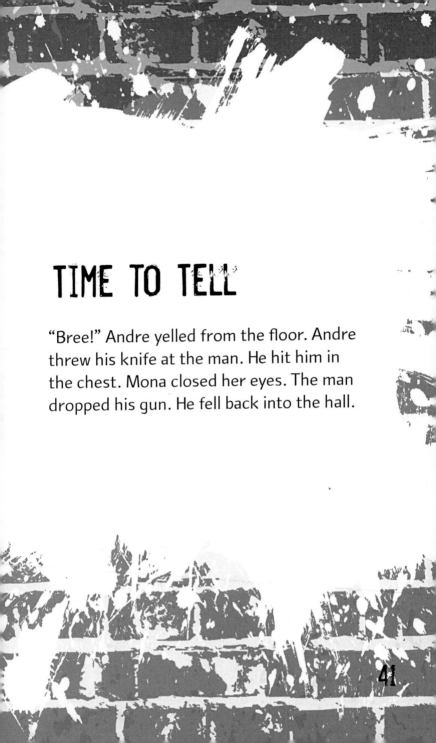

TIME TO TELL

"Bree!" Andre yelled from the floor. Andre threw his knife at the man. He hit him in the chest. Mona closed her eyes. The man dropped his gun. He fell back into the hall.

Mr. Edwin ran at Bree and Mona. Bree turned and fired the gun at him. The bullet hit him in the chest. He fell to the floor. Dead.

Bree and Mona and Andre heard something outside the window. The police.

The police came to apartment 4A. They found the dead body of the man in the hall. The knife was in his chest. They found Mr. Edwin's dead body.

Bree told the police about working for Mr. Edwin. She told them about delivering the boxes. "He came here looking for a box," Bree told them. "He tried to kill us for it."

"Did you know what was in the boxes you were delivering?" the policeman asked.

"No," Bree replied.

The police talked to Mona. Mona did not tell the police that she knew about the drugs. Mona defended Bree to the police. "Mr. Edwin and his driver tried to kill us," Mona said. "Bree and Andre had to protect us."

The police talked to Andre. He told them about using his knife to save Bree. The police called an ambulance for him. His leg was still bleeding.

"I'll be okay," he said to Bree. "Don't worry about me." The ambulance took Andre to the hospital.

No one told the police about seeing Tutu's ghost.

The police also went into apartment 4B. Bree knew she had to tell the police about their aunt. She knew she had to tell them she was dead. Bree told the police that Andre took their aunt's body.

"I don't know where he took it," Bree said. "She died on her own. I was with her. I saw it. We didn't kill her."

Bree knew the police would arrest Andre at the hospital. She did not want that to happen, but she knew it would.

THE BODY

Andre sat in a hospital bed after the bullet was removed from his leg. The police asked about his aunt's dead body. "We think we know why you did it," the policeman said. "Where's the body? Tell us."

Andre told them he buried her body in the woods outside the city limits. He gave them directions.

"You don't own a car," the policeman said. "Who helped you with the body?"

"A friend," Andre replied.

"Give us a name."

"I'll never do that."

"It was really Bree, wasn't it?"

"No," Andre replied. "She had nothing to do with it."

The police found his aunt's body. Andre went to jail. He couldn't make bail. The police tested the body. She died from old age.

Andre never told the police who helped him move the body. The judge in his case did not like that.

Andre's lawyer tried to help him. "You have a past drug charge," she said. "The judge may give you more jail time."

The lawyer was right. The judge sentenced Andre to a year in jail.

NO MORE LIES

Bree visited Andre after his first month in jail. She could see a change in him. He was different with her when he was sober.

"How's your leg?" Bree asked.

"It's good," Andre replied. "It's getting better."

"That's good," Bree said.

"So, where do you live now?" Andre asked.

"I'm living with Mona and her kids for now."

They looked at each other and did not speak. Then Andre broke the silence. "Did you tell the police about Mama?" Andre asked.

"No. What could I say? If I told them about her ghost, they would lock me up."

Andre and Bree smiled at each other.

"I still can't understand what I saw," Andre said. "Was it *really* her?"

"Yes, the ghost of Tutu was real," Bree replied. "And she saved our lives. I think that's why she came back. To save us."

They looked at each other.

Bree sighed. "What are you going to do when you get out?" she asked.

"I don't know. Promise me something."

"What?"

"Promise me you'll never work for guys like Edwin again."

"I promise," Bree said.

"Or live with a guy like Edwin," Andre said.

"I promise," Bree said with a smile.

"Or marry a guy like Edwin," he said as he smiled back.

"I promise," Bree said.

"Or have kids with a guy like Edwin," he said.

"I promise!"

NEW START

"Mommy has to go to work. Be good for Auntie Bree," Mona said to her kids. "Did I give you my shopping list?" Mona asked Bree.

"Yes, I have it," Bree replied. "Now go, or you'll be late."

"Okay, thanks," Mona replied as she closed the front door.

"Auntie Bree!" Mona's son called out. "I want cereal for breakfast!"

Bree moved in with Mona and her children. Bree took care of them. She did not have to pay for food or rent. The kids were fun. And Bree was good with them.

Mona found a new job. She managed an office and made more money. Mona liked her new job and boss. She was happy Bree was with her kids while she was at work.

Bree studied at night for her GED. She wanted to finish high school so she could go to college. She had a new family and home. Bree was happy.

Sometimes before she fell asleep, Bree would think about her mother. But she never saw Tutu's ghost again.

ABOUT THE AUTHOR

PJ Gray is a versatile, award-winning freelance writer experienced in short stories, essays, and feature writing. He is a former managing editor for *Pride* magazine, a ghost writer, blogger, researcher, food writer, and cookbook author. He currently resides in Chicago, Illinois. For more information about PJ Gray, go to www.pjgray.com.